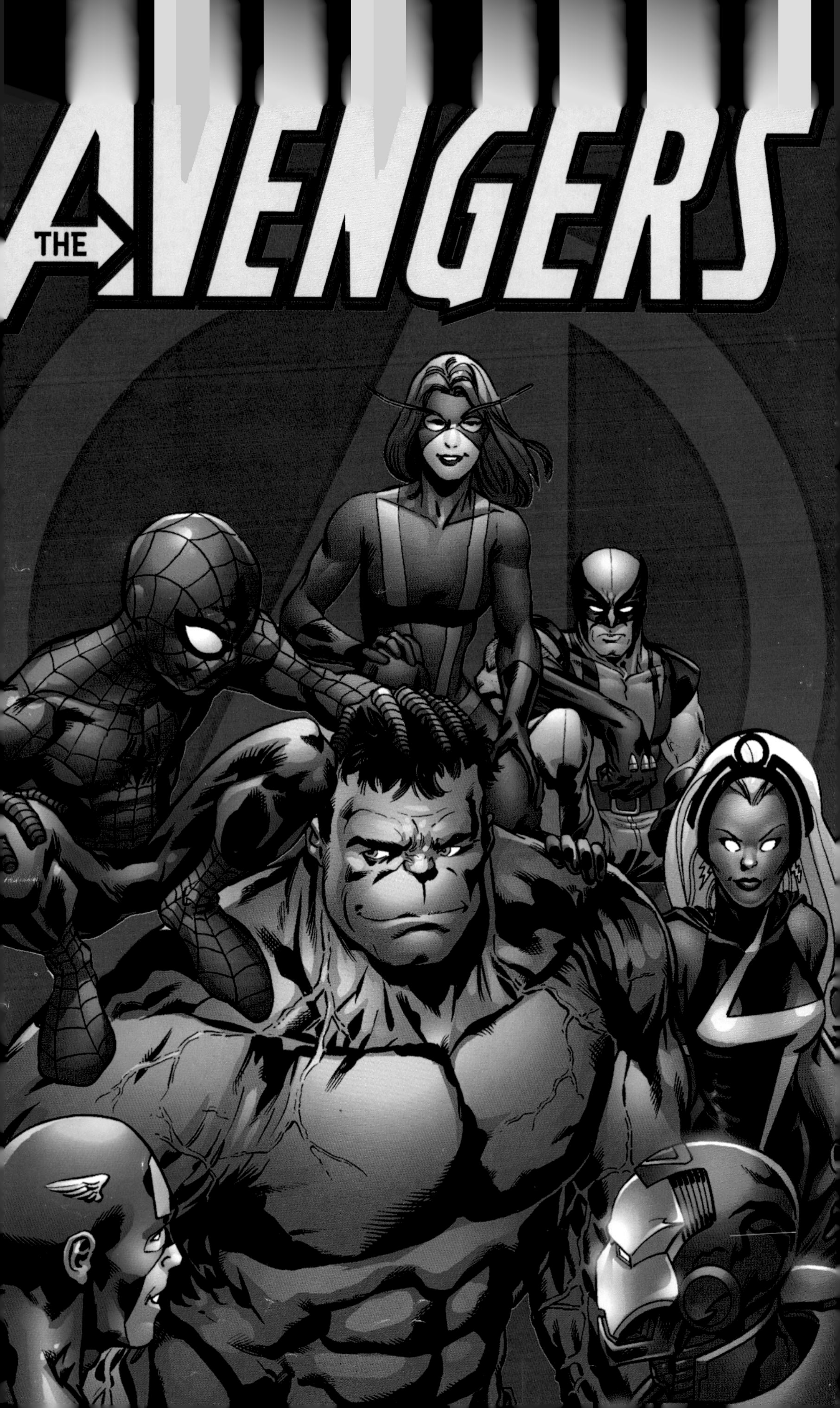
THE AVENGERS

VISIT US AT
www.abdopublishing.com

Reinforced library bound edition published in 2011 by Spotlight, a division of the ABDO Group, 8000 West 78th Street, Edina, Minnesota 55439. Spotlight produces high-quality reinforced library bound editions for schools and libraries. Published by agreement with Marvel Characters, Inc.

Printed in the United States of America, Melrose Park, Illinois.
042010
092010
This book contains at least 10% recycled material.

Library of Congress Cataloging-in-Publication Data

Tobin, Paul.
  Doll winners squad / story, Paul Tobin ; art, Dario Brizuela.
     p. cm. -- (The Avengers)
  "Marvel."
  ISBN 978-1-59961-766-4
  1. Graphic novels. I. Brizuela, Dario, ill. II. Avengers (Comic strip) III. Title.
  PZ7.7.T62Dol 2010
  741.5'973--dc22
                    2009052831

All Spotlight books have reinforced library bindings and
are manufactured in the United States of America.

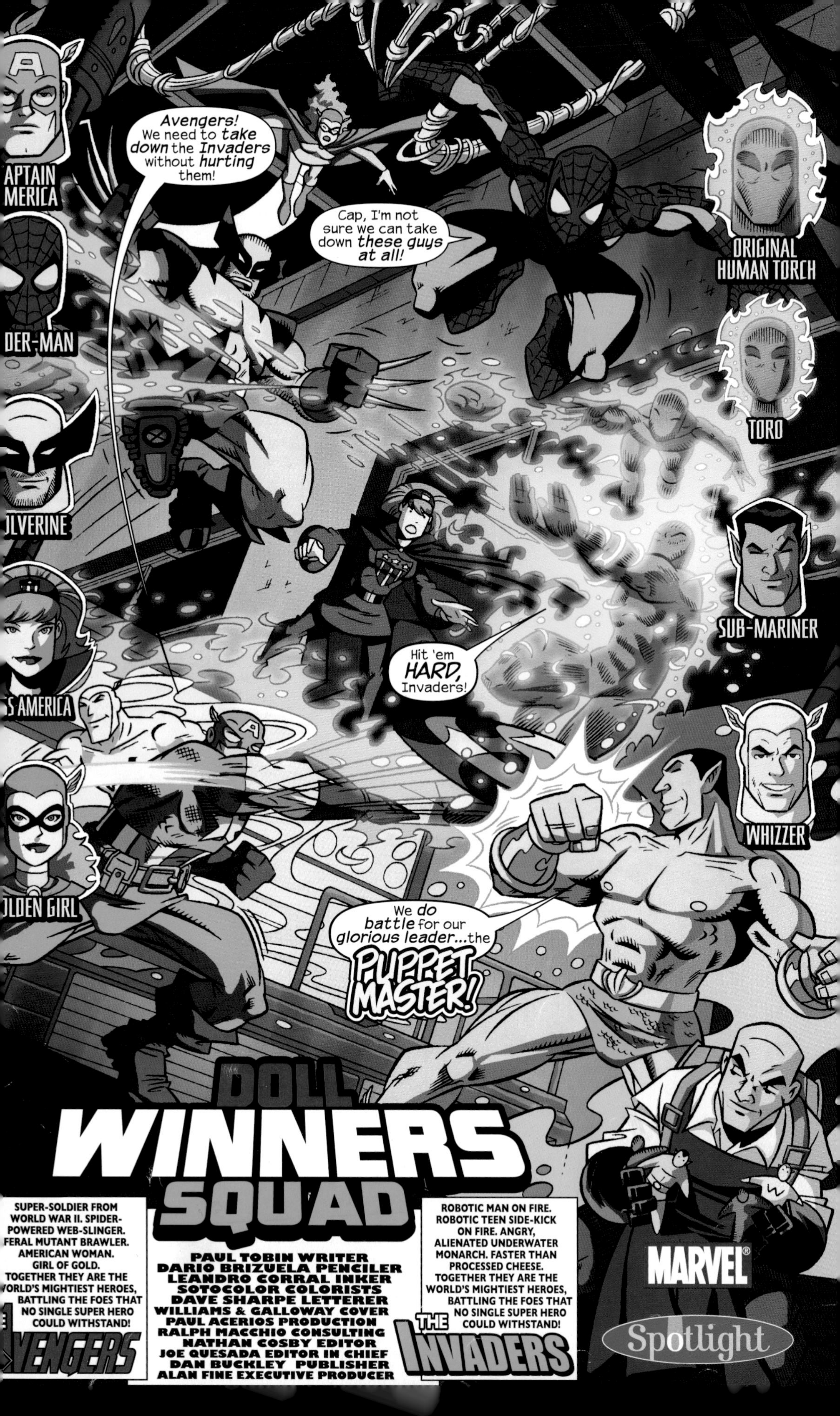
APTAIN MERICA
DER-MAN
LVERINE
S AMERICA
OLDEN GIRL
ORIGINAL HUMAN TORCH
TORO
SUB-MARINER
WHIZZER
Avengers! We need to take down the Invaders without hurting them!
Cap, I'm not sure we can take down these guys at all!
Hit 'em HARD, Invaders!
We do battle for our glorious leader...the PUPPET MASTER!
DOLL
WINNERS
SQUAD
SUPER-SOLDIER FROM WORLD WAR II. SPIDER-POWERED WEB-SLINGER. FERAL MUTANT BRAWLER. AMERICAN WOMAN. GIRL OF GOLD. TOGETHER THEY ARE THE ORLD'S MIGHTIEST HEROES, BATTLING THE FOES THAT NO SINGLE SUPER HERO COULD WITHSTAND!
VENGERS
PAUL TOBIN WRITER
DARIO BRIZUELA PENCILER
LEANDRO CORRAL INKER
SOTOCOLOR COLORISTS
DAVE SHARPE LETTERER
WILLIAMS & GALLOWAY COVER
PAUL ACERIOS PRODUCTION
RALPH MACCHIO CONSULTING
NATHAN COSBY EDITOR
JOE QUESADA EDITOR IN CHIEF
DAN BUCKLEY PUBLISHER
ALAN FINE EXECUTIVE PRODUCER
ROBOTIC MAN ON FIRE. ROBOTIC TEEN SIDE-KICK ON FIRE. ANGRY, ALIENATED UNDERWATER MONARCH. FASTER THAN PROCESSED CHEESE. TOGETHER THEY ARE THE WORLD'S MIGHTIEST HEROES, BATTLING THE FOES THAT NO SINGLE SUPER HERO COULD WITHSTAND!
THE INVADERS
MARVEL®
Spotlight

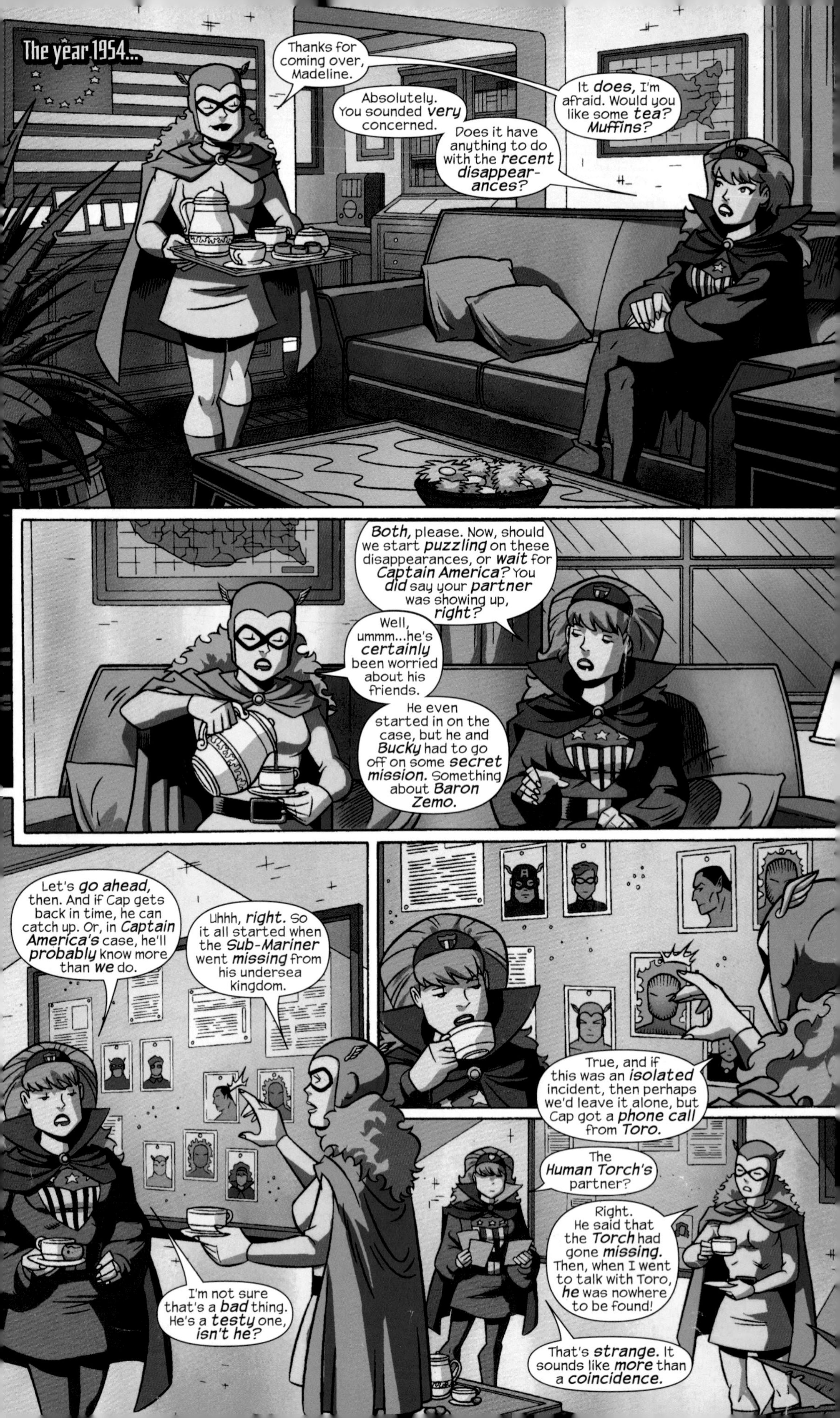
The year 1954...
Thanks for coming over, Madeline.
Absolutely. You sounded very concerned.
Does it have anything to do with the recent disappear-ances?
It does, I'm afraid. Would you like some tea? Muffins?
Both, please. Now, should we start puzzling on these disappearances, or wait for Captain America? You did say your partner was showing up, right?
Well, ummm...he's certainly been worried about his friends.
He even started in on the case, but he and Bucky had to go off on some secret mission. Something about Baron Zemo.
Let's go ahead, then. And if Cap gets back in time, he can catch up. Or, in Captain America's case, he'll probably know more than we do.
Uhhh, right. So it all started when the Sub-Mariner went missing from his undersea kingdom.
I'm not sure that's a bad thing. He's a testy one, isn't he?
True, and if this was an isolated incident, then perhaps we'd leave it alone, but Cap got a phone call from Toro.
The Human Torch's partner?
Right. He said that the Torch had gone missing. Then, when I went to talk with Toro, he was nowhere to be found!
That's strange. It sounds like more than a coincidence.

What does *Captain America* think of all this?

Captain America is... *gone?*

Keep this very quiet, but Cap and Bucky have gone missing as well.

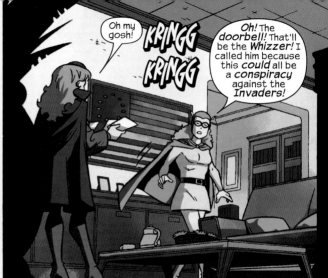

Oh my gosh!

KRINGG KRINGG

Oh! The *doorbell!* That'll be the *Whizzer!* I called him because this *could* all be a *conspiracy* against the *Invaders!*

Afternoon, *Golden Girl.* I got here as *fast* as I could.

And for *me,* that's pretty--

Oh!

He's *gone!*

There's some sort of *odd disturbance* here in the air! My hand just *disappears!*

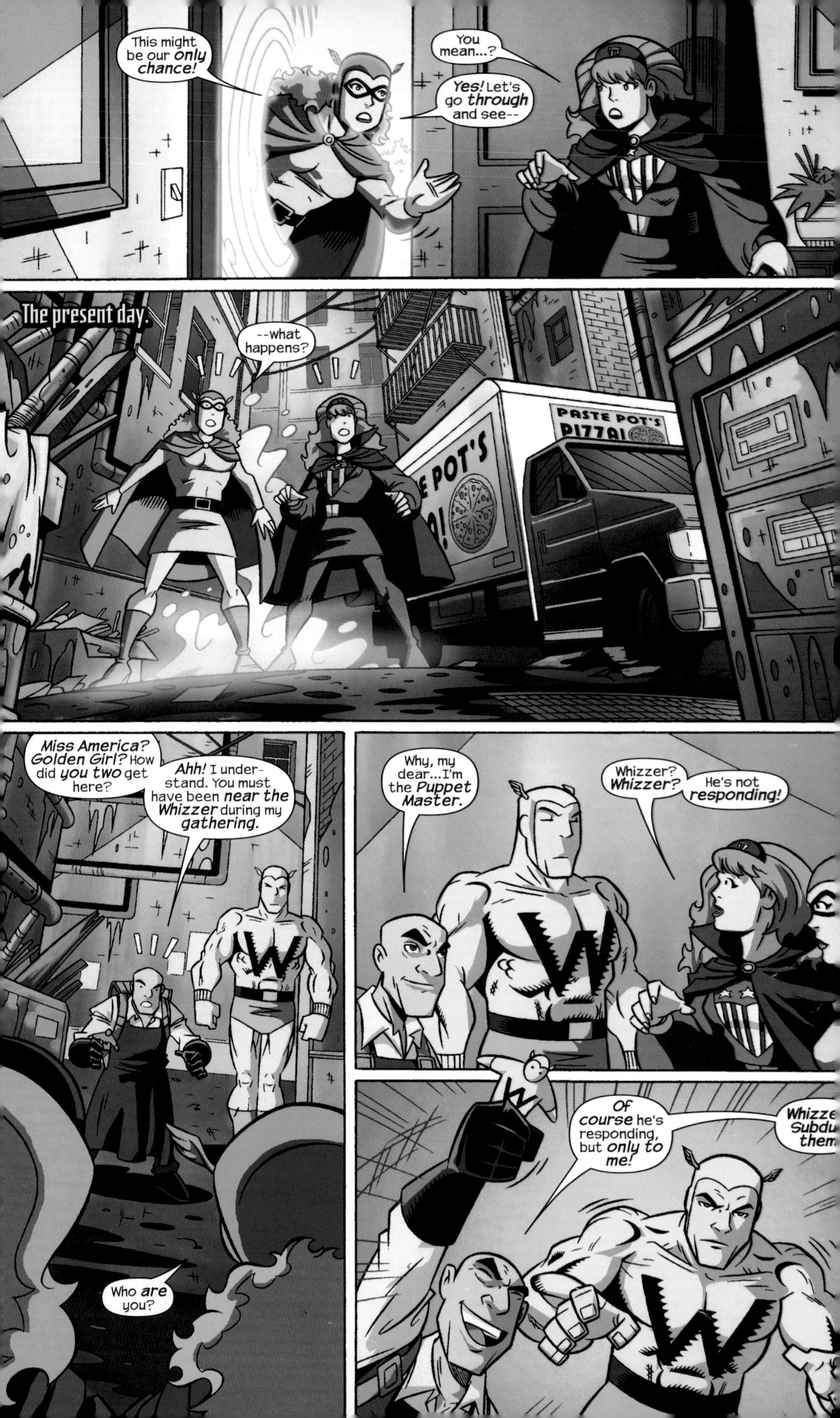

This might be our only chance!
You mean...?
Yes! Let's go through and see--
The present day.
--what happens?
PASTE POT'S PIZZA!
PASTE POT'S
Miss America? Golden Girl? How did you two get here?
Ahh! I understand. You must have been near the Whizzer during my gathering.
Who are you?
Why, my dear...I'm the Puppet Master.
Whizzer? Whizzer?
He's not responding!
Of course he's responding, but only to me!

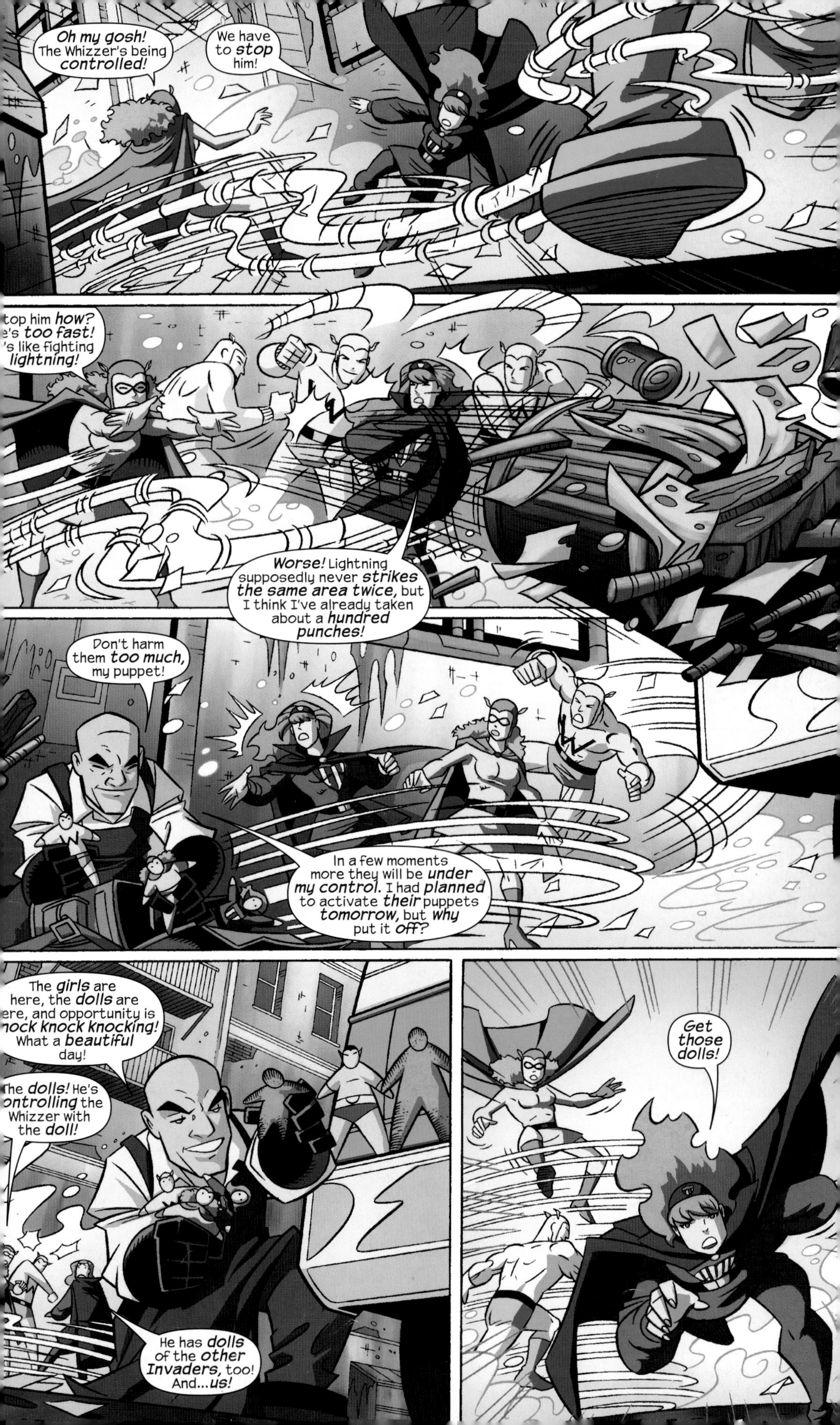
Oh my gosh! The Whizzer's being controlled!
We have to stop him!
top him how? e's too fast! 's like fighting lightning!
Worse! Lightning supposedly never strikes the same area twice, but I think I've already taken about a hundred punches!
Don't harm them too much, my puppet!
In a few moments more they will be under my control. I had planned to activate their puppets tomorrow, but why put it off?
The girls are here, the dolls are ere, and opportunity is nock knock knocking! What a beautiful day!
The dolls! He's ontrolling the Whizzer with the doll!
He has dolls of the other Invaders, too! And...us!
Get those dolls!

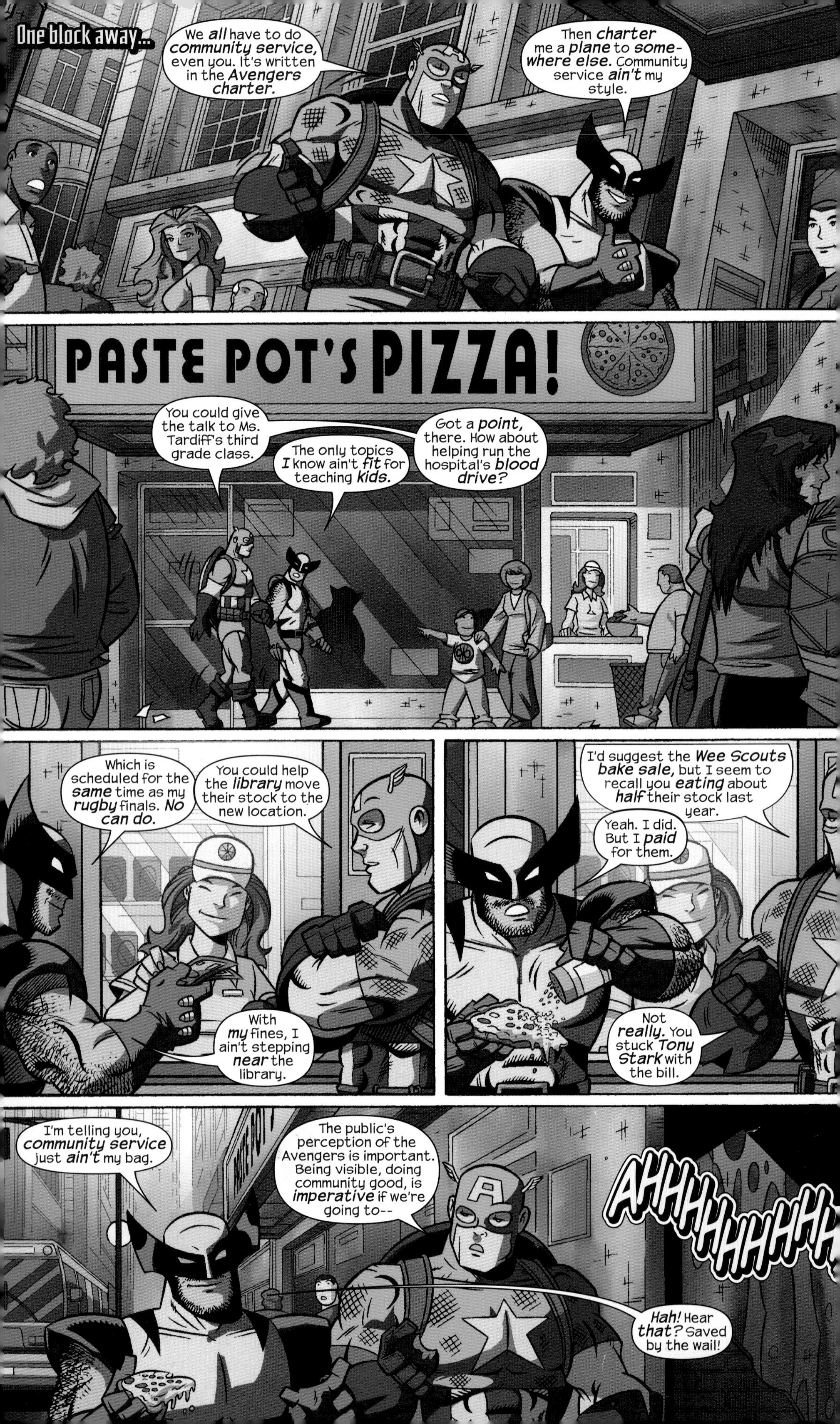

One block away...
We all have to do community service, even you. It's written in the Avengers charter.
Then charter me a plane to somewhere else. Community service ain't my style.
PASTE POT'S PIZZA!
You could give the talk to Ms. Tardiff's third grade class.
The only topics I know ain't fit for teaching kids.
Got a point, there. How about helping run the hospital's blood drive?
Which is scheduled for the same time as my rugby finals. No can do.
You could help the library move their stock to the new location.
With my fines, I ain't stepping near the library.
I'd suggest the Wee Scouts bake sale, but I seem to recall you eating about half their stock last year.
Yeah. I did. But I paid for them.
Not really. You stuck Tony Stark with the bill.
I'm telling you, community service just ain't my bag.
The public's perception of the Avengers is important. Being visible, doing community good, is imperative if we're going to--
AHHHHHHHHHH
Hah! Hear that? Saved by the wail!

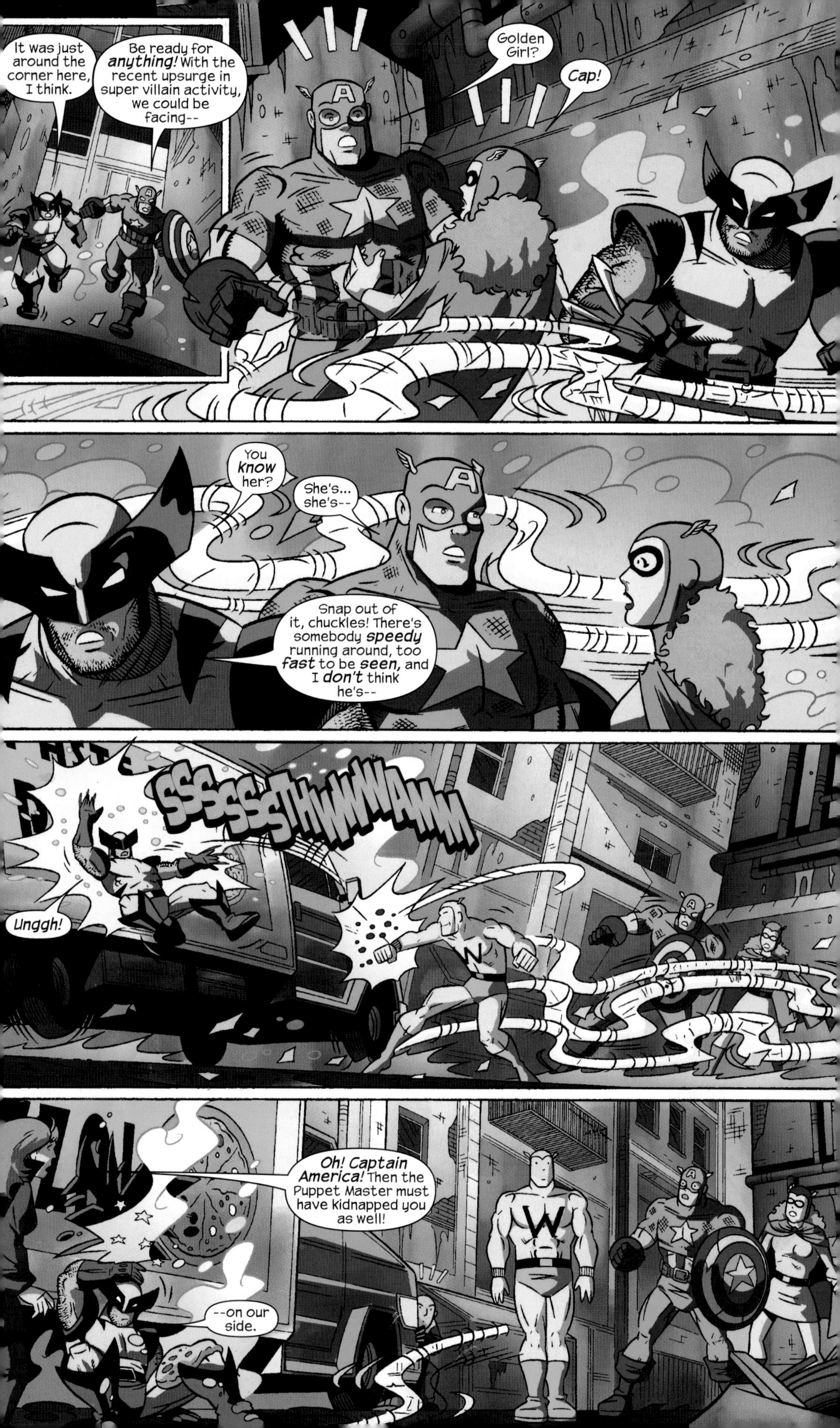
It was just around the corner here, I think.
Be ready for anything! With the recent upsurge in super villain activity, we could be facing--
Golden Girl?
Cap!
You know her?
She's... she's--
Snap out of it, chuckles! There's somebody speedy running around, too fast to be seen, and I don't think he's--
SSSSSSTHWWWAMM
Unggh!
Oh! Captain America! Then the Puppet Master must have kidnapped you as well!
--on our side.

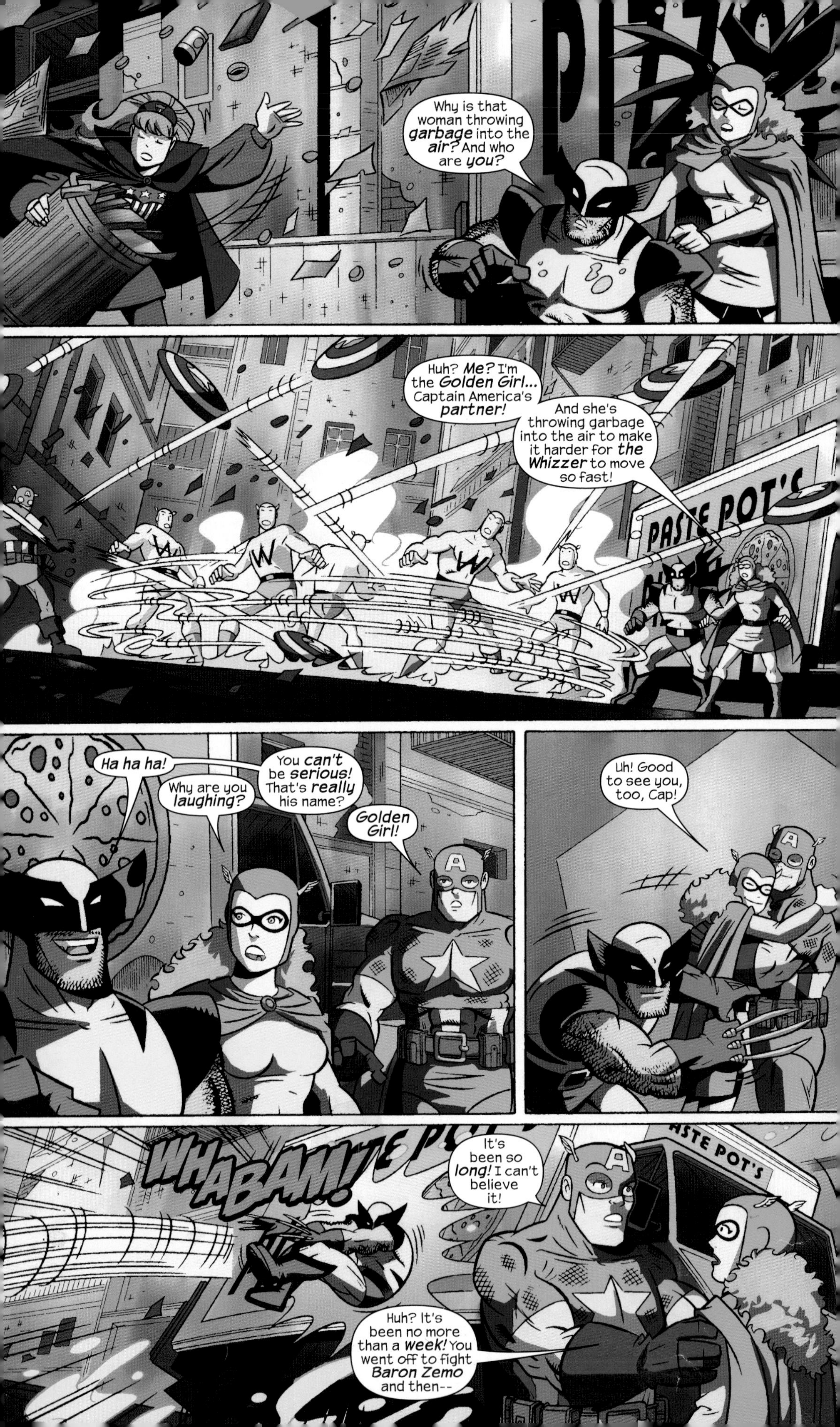

Why is that woman throwing garbage into the air? And who are you?
Huh? Me? I'm the Golden Girl... Captain America's partner!
And she's throwing garbage into the air to make it harder for the Whizzer to move so fast!
PASTE POT'S
Ha ha ha!
Why are you laughing?
You can't be serious! That's really his name?
Golden Girl!
Uh! Good to see you, too, Cap!
WHABAM!
PASTE POT'S
It's been so long! I can't believe it!
Huh? It's been no more than a week! You went off to fight Baron Zemo and then--

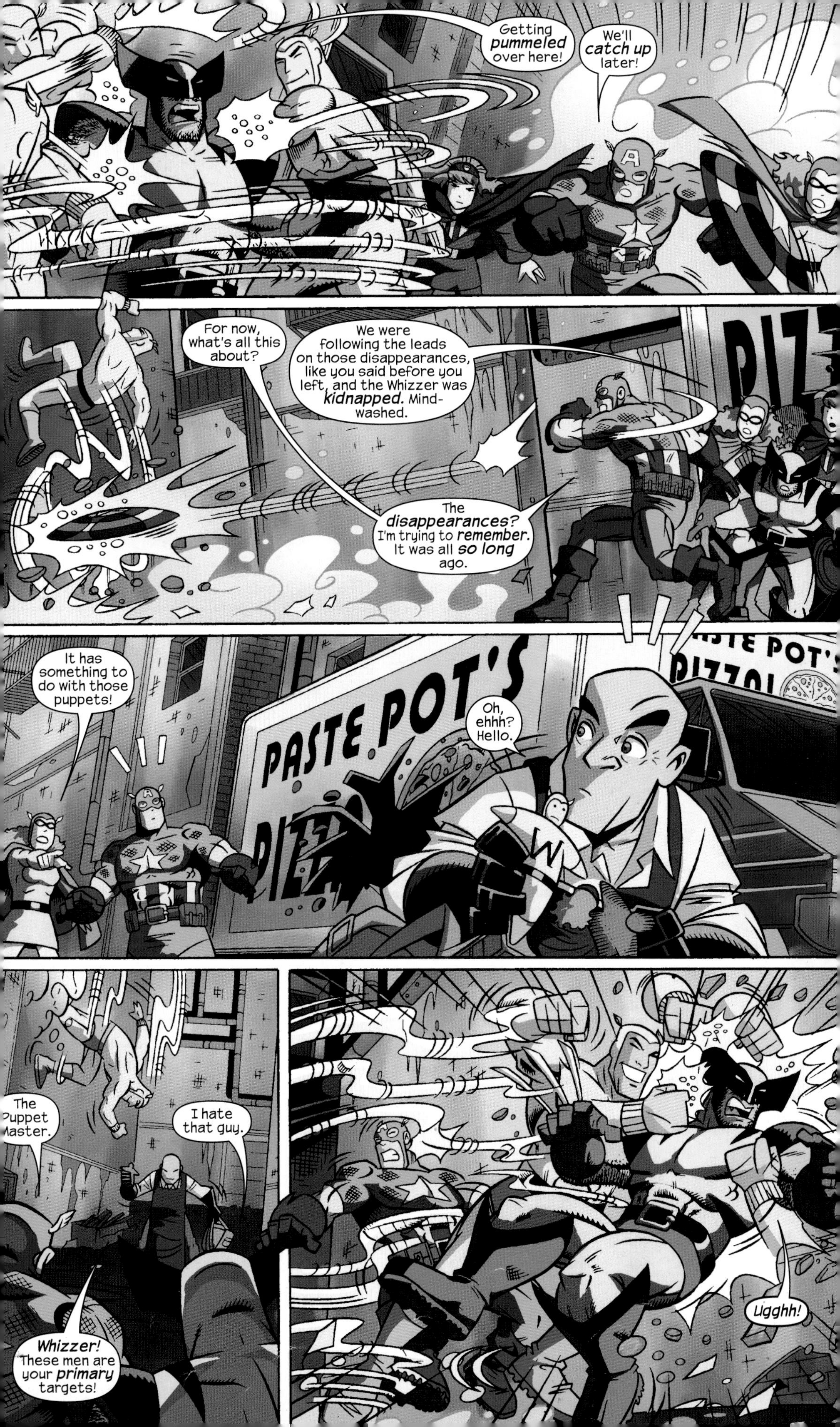

Getting *pummeled* over here!
We'll *catch up* later!
For now, what's all this about?
We were following the leads on those disappearances, like you said before you left, and the Whizzer was *kidnapped.* Mind-washed.
The *disappearances?* I'm trying to *remember.* It was all *so long* ago.
PIZZ
It has something to do with those puppets!
PASTE POT'S PIZZA
Oh, ehhh? Hello.
The Puppet Master.
I hate that guy.
Whizzer! These men are your *primary* targets!
Ugghh!

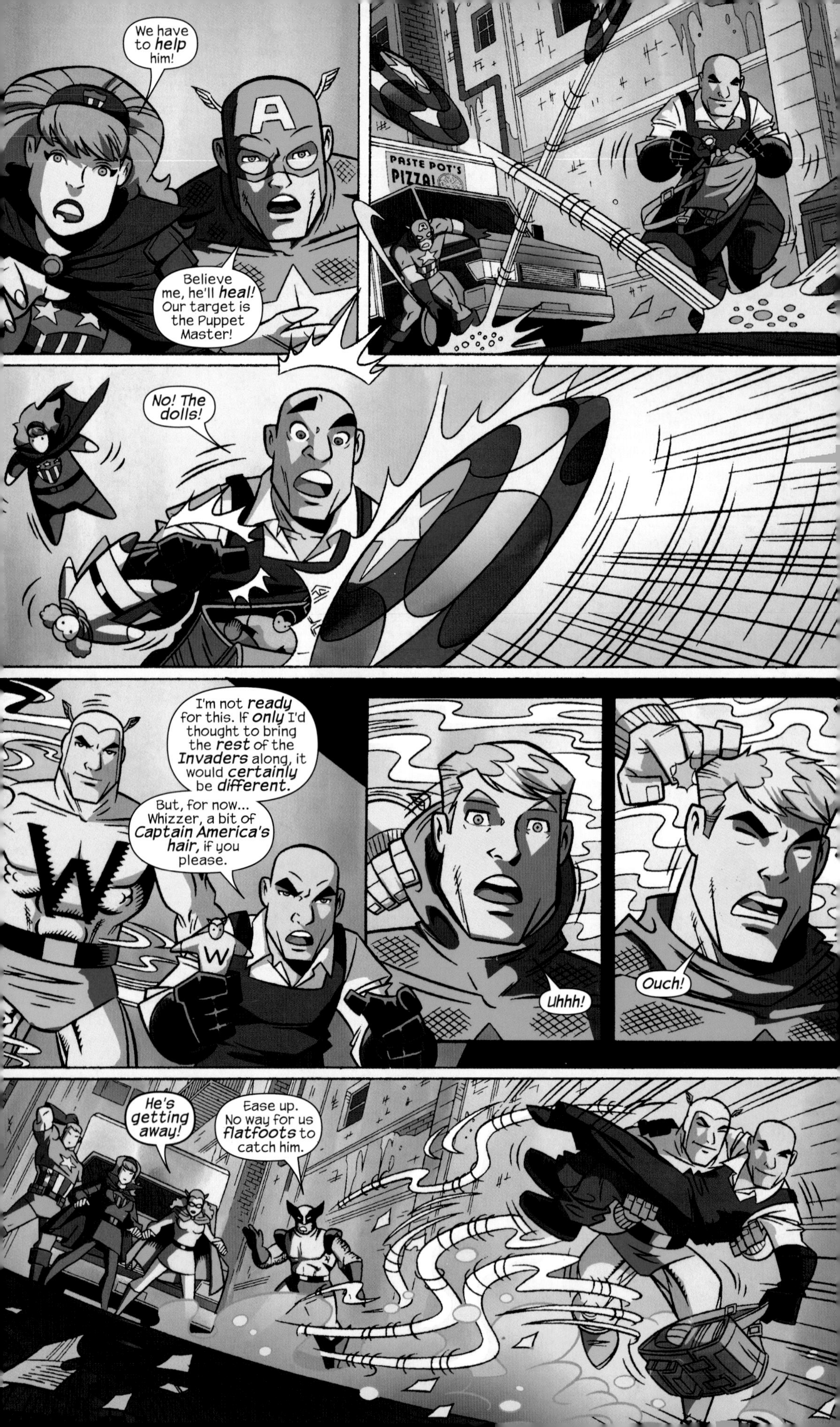

We have to *help* him!
Believe me, he'll *heal!* Our target is the Puppet Master!
PASTE POT'S PIZZA!
No! The dolls!
I'm not *ready* for this. If *only* I'd thought to bring the *rest* of the *Invaders* along, it would *certainly* be *different.*
But, for now... Whizzer, a bit of *Captain America's hair,* if you please.
Uhhh!
Ouch!
He's getting away!
Ease up. No way for us *flatfoots* to catch him.

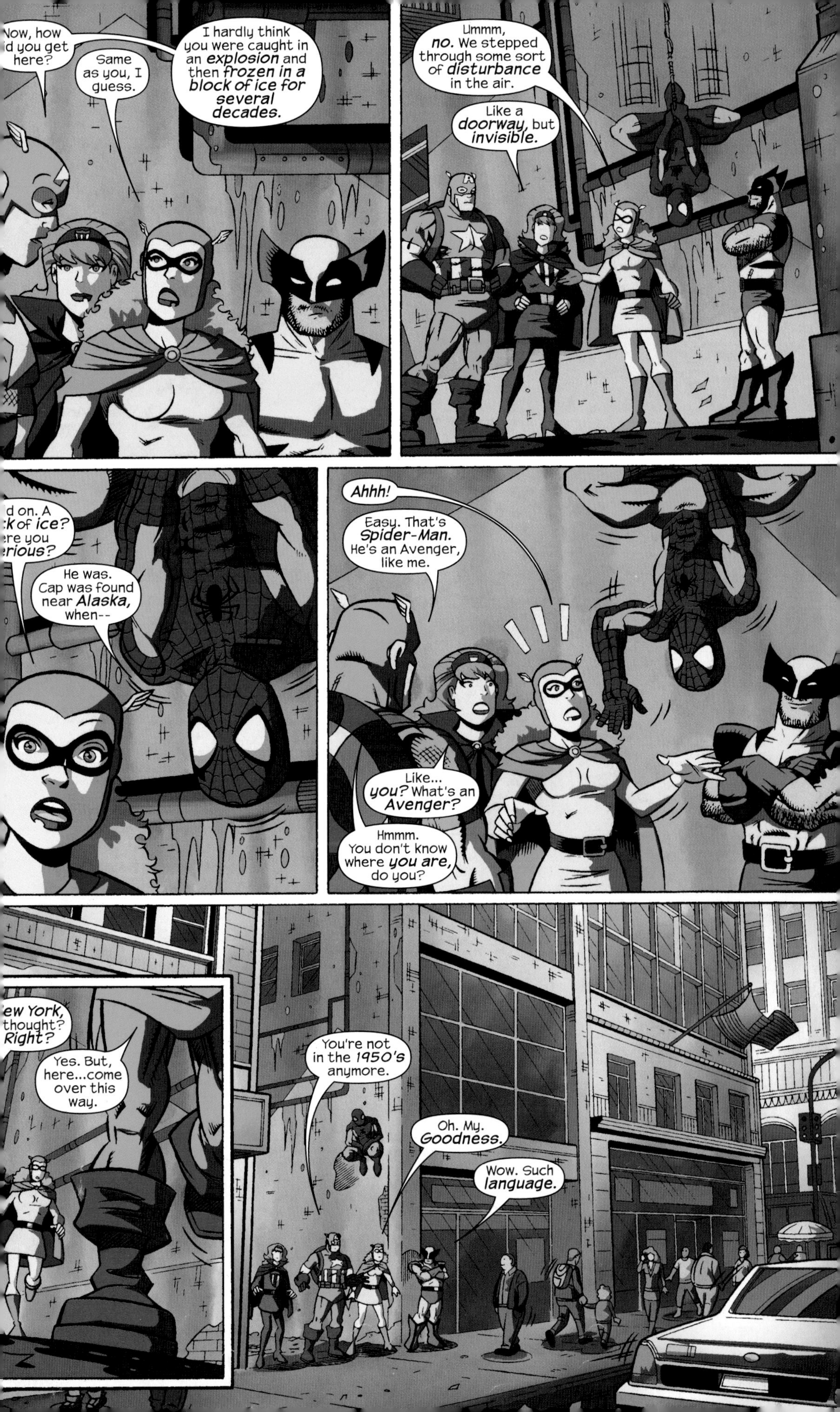

Now, how d you get here?
Same as you, I guess.
I hardly think you were caught in an *explosion* and then *frozen in a block of ice for several decades.*
Ummm, *no.* We stepped through some sort of *disturbance* in the air.
Like a *doorway,* but *invisible.*
d on. A k of *ice?* re you rious?
He was. Cap was found near *Alaska,* when--
Ahhh!
Easy. That's *Spider-Man.* He's an Avenger, like me.
Like... *you?* What's an *Avenger?*
Hmmm. You don't know where *you are,* do you?
ew York, thought? *Right?*
Yes. But, here...come over this way.
You're not in the *1950's* anymore.
Oh. My. *Goodness.*
Wow. Such *language.*

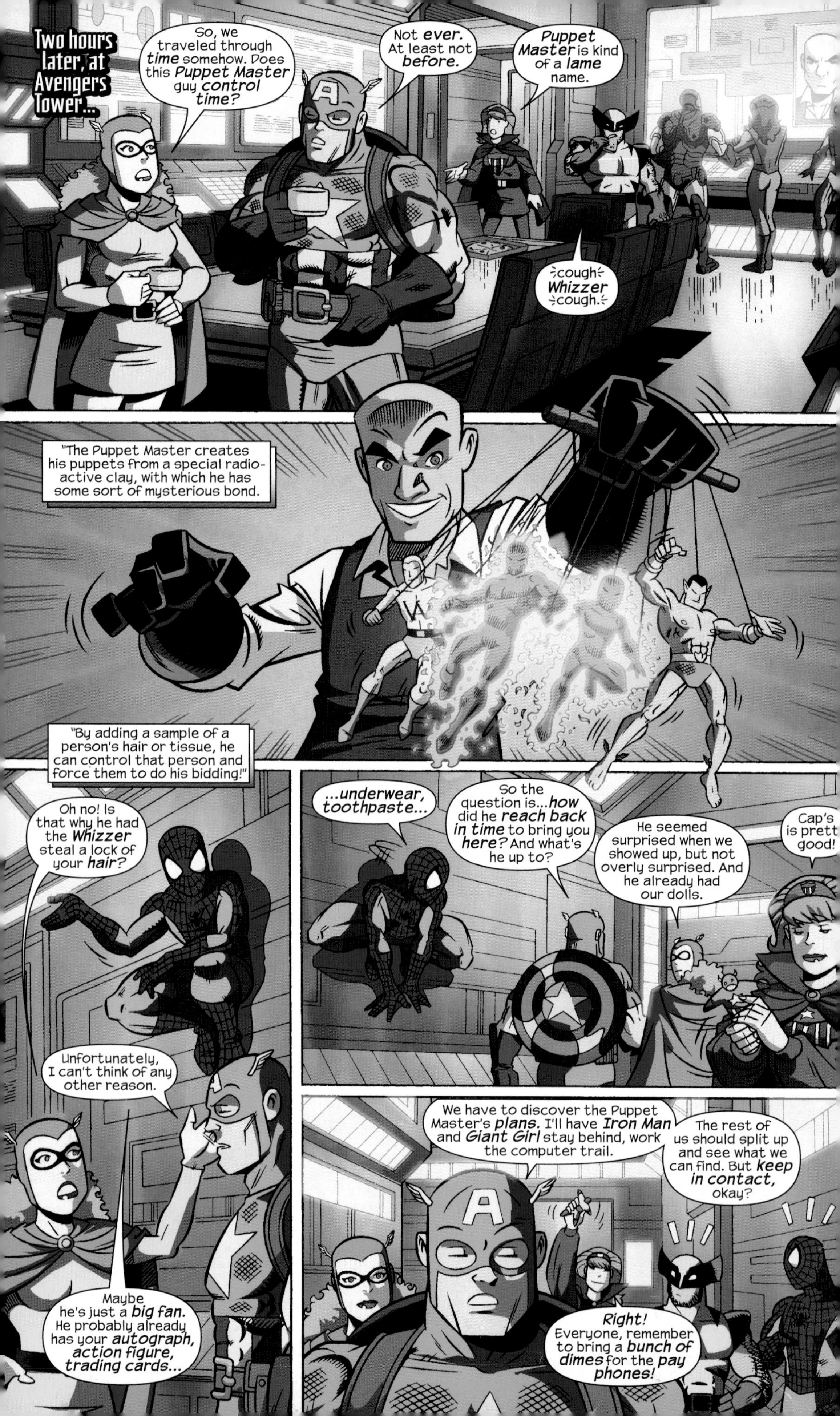
Two hours later, at Avengers Tower...
So, we traveled through time somehow. Does this Puppet Master guy control time?
Not ever. At least not before.
Puppet Master is kind of a lame name.
cough Whizzer cough.
"The Puppet Master creates his puppets from a special radio-active clay, with which he has some sort of mysterious bond.
"By adding a sample of a person's hair or tissue, he can control that person and force them to do his bidding!"
Oh no! Is that why he had the Whizzer steal a lock of your hair?
Unfortunately, I can't think of any other reason.
Maybe he's just a big fan. He probably already has your autograph, action figure, trading cards...
...underwear, toothpaste...
So the question is...how did he reach back in time to bring you here? And what's he up to?
He seemed surprised when we showed up, but not overly surprised. And he already had our dolls.
Cap's is prett good!
We have to discover the Puppet Master's plans. I'll have Iron Man and Giant Girl stay behind, work the computer trail.
The rest of us should split up and see what we can find. But keep in contact, okay?
Right! Everyone, remember to bring a bunch of dimes for the pay phones!

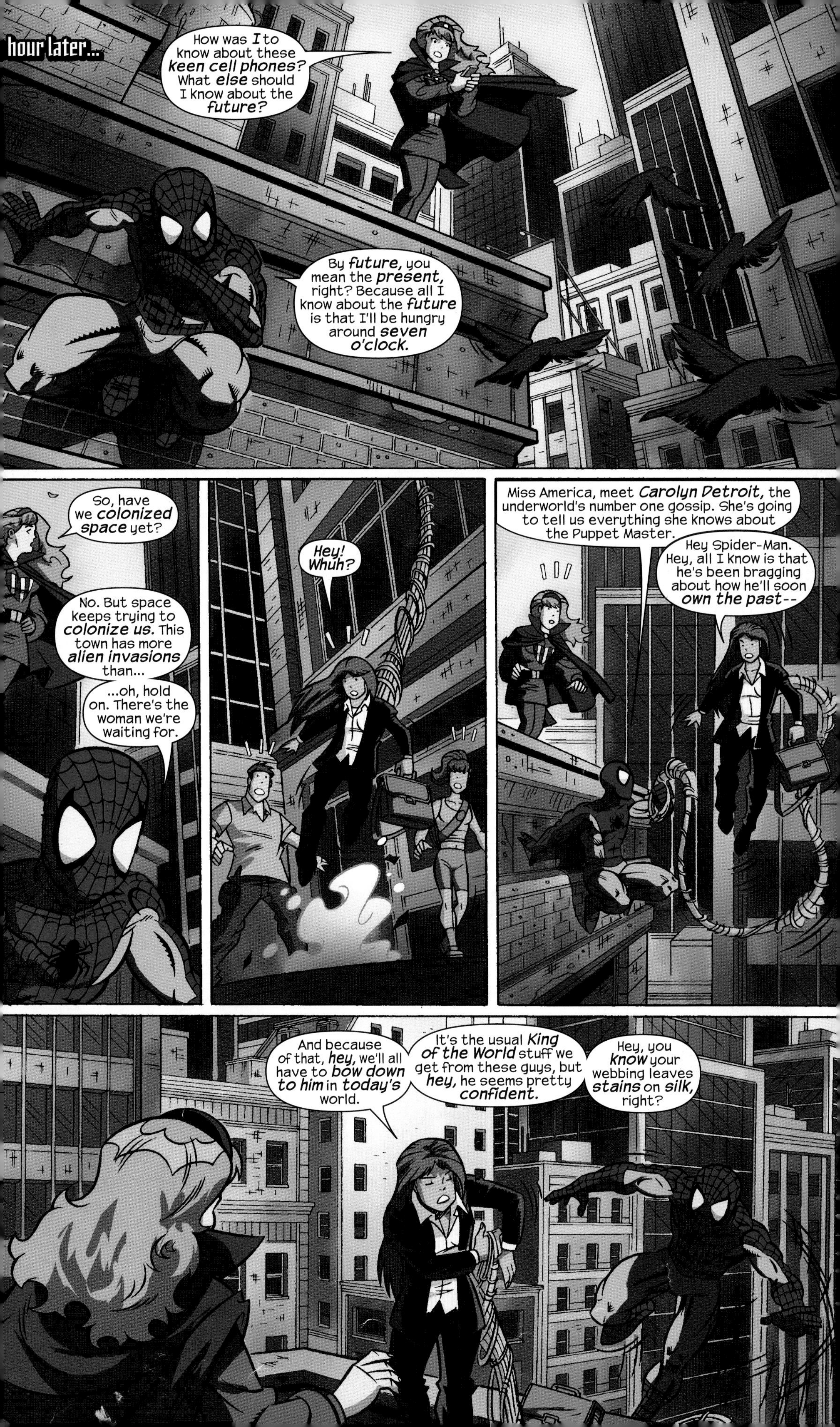
hour later...
How was I to know about these keen cell phones? What else should I know about the future?
By future, you mean the present, right? Because all I know about the future is that I'll be hungry around seven o'clock.
So, have we colonized space yet?
No. But space keeps trying to colonize us. This town has more alien invasions than...
...oh, hold on. There's the woman we're waiting for.
Hey! Whuh?
Miss America, meet Carolyn Detroit, the underworld's number one gossip. She's going to tell us everything she knows about the Puppet Master.
Hey Spider-Man. Hey, all I know is that he's been bragging about how he'll soon own the past--
And because of that, hey, we'll all have to bow down to him in today's world.
It's the usual King of the World stuff we get from these guys, but hey, he seems pretty confident.
Hey, you know your webbing leaves stains on silk, right?

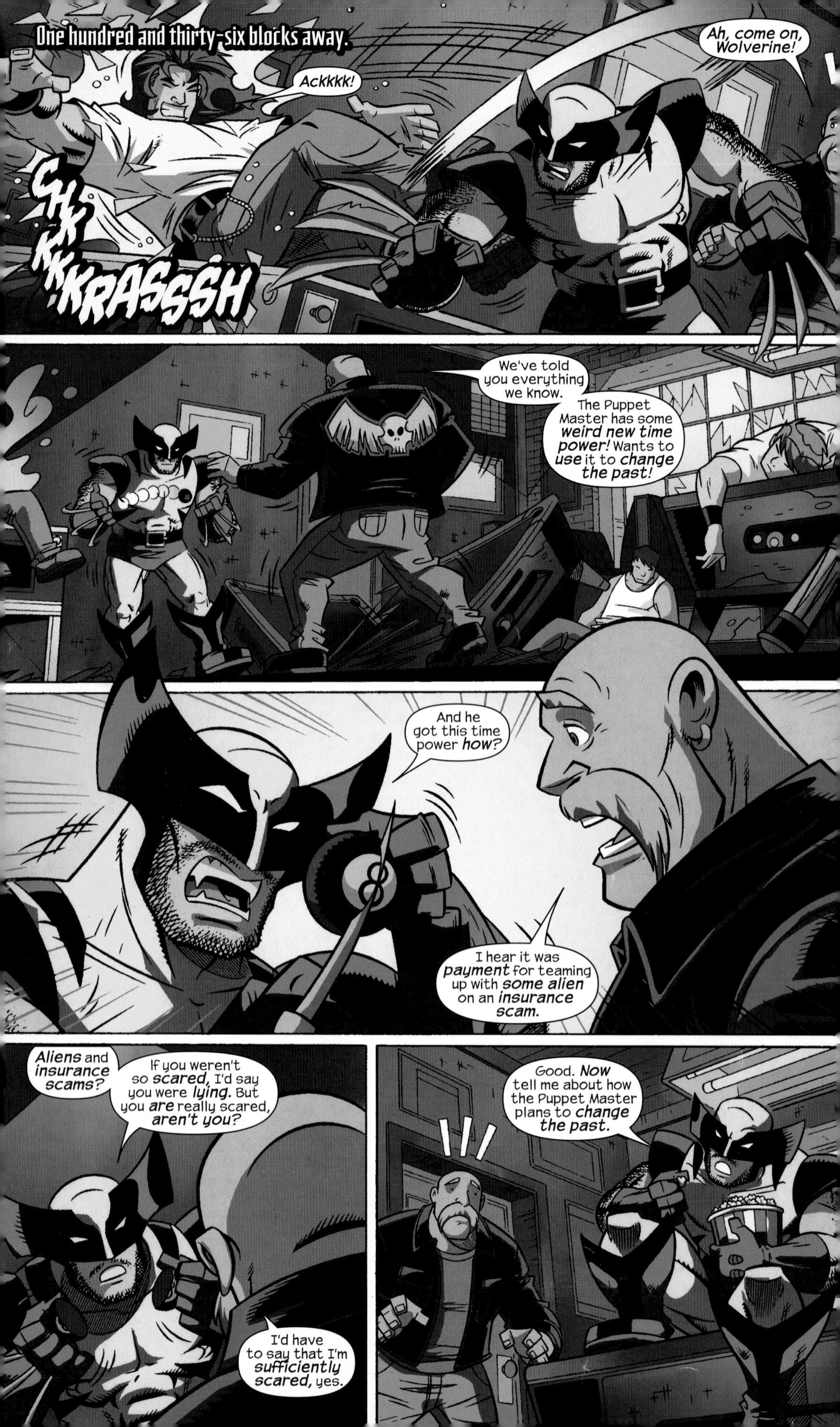

One hundred and thirty-six blocks away.
Ackkkk!
Ah, come on, Wolverine!
CHKKKKRASSSH
We've told you everything we know.
The Puppet Master has some weird new time power! Wants to use it to change the past!
And he got this time power how?
I hear it was payment for teaming up with some alien on an insurance scam.
Aliens and insurance scams?
If you weren't so scared, I'd say you were lying. But you are really scared, aren't you?
I'd have to say that I'm sufficiently scared, yes.
Good. Now tell me about how the Puppet Master plans to change the past.

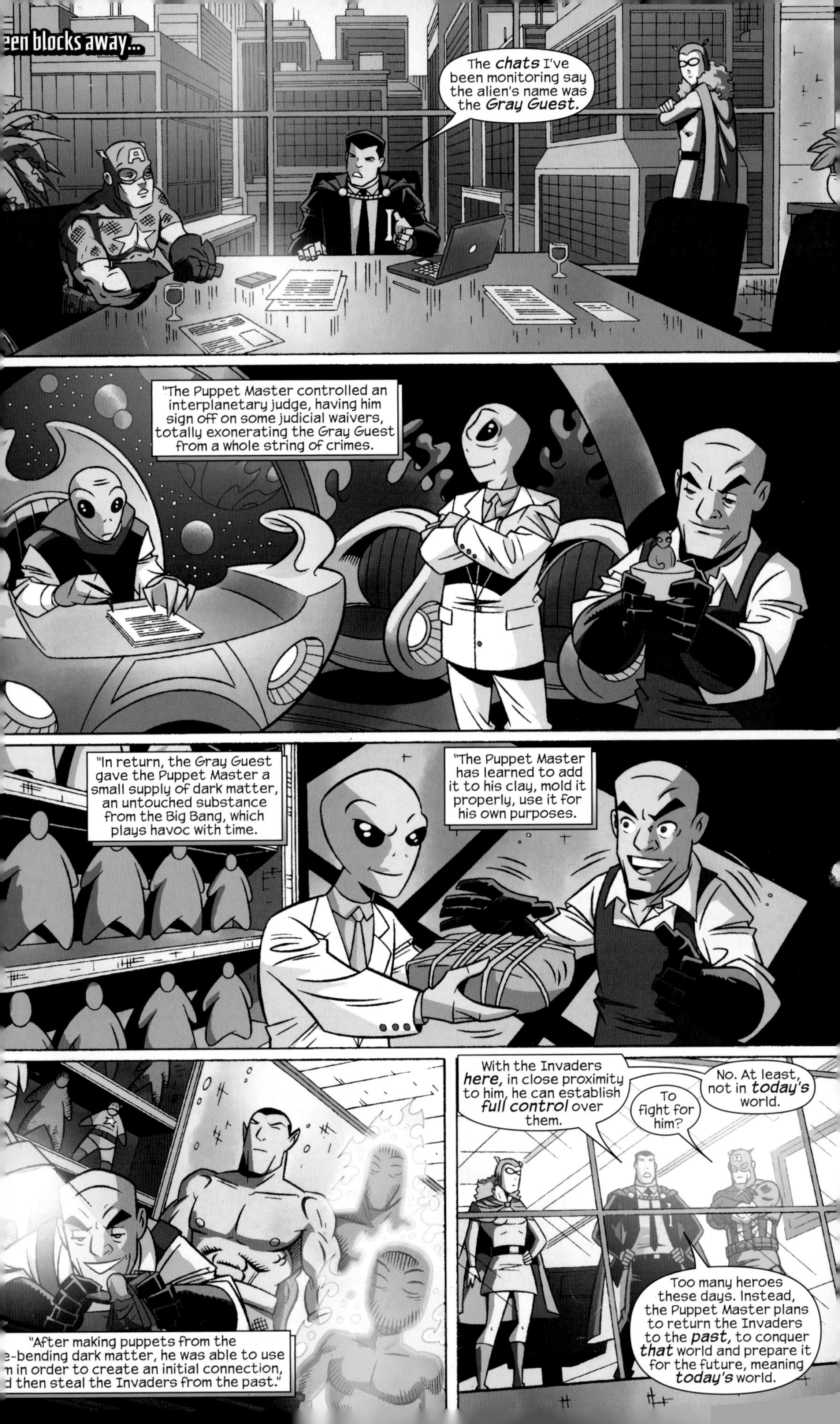
een blocks away...
The chats I've been monitoring say the alien's name was the Gray Guest.
"The Puppet Master controlled an interplanetary judge, having him sign off on some judicial waivers, totally exonerating the Gray Guest from a whole string of crimes.
"In return, the Gray Guest gave the Puppet Master a small supply of dark matter, an untouched substance from the Big Bang, which plays havoc with time.
"The Puppet Master has learned to add it to his clay, mold it properly, use it for his own purposes.
"After making puppets from the
e-bending dark matter, he was able to use
n in order to create an initial connection,
d then steal the Invaders from the past."
With the Invaders here, in close proximity to him, he can establish full control over them.
To fight for him?
No. At least, not in today's world.
Too many heroes these days. Instead, the Puppet Master plans to return the Invaders to the past, to conquer that world and prepare it for the future, meaning today's world.

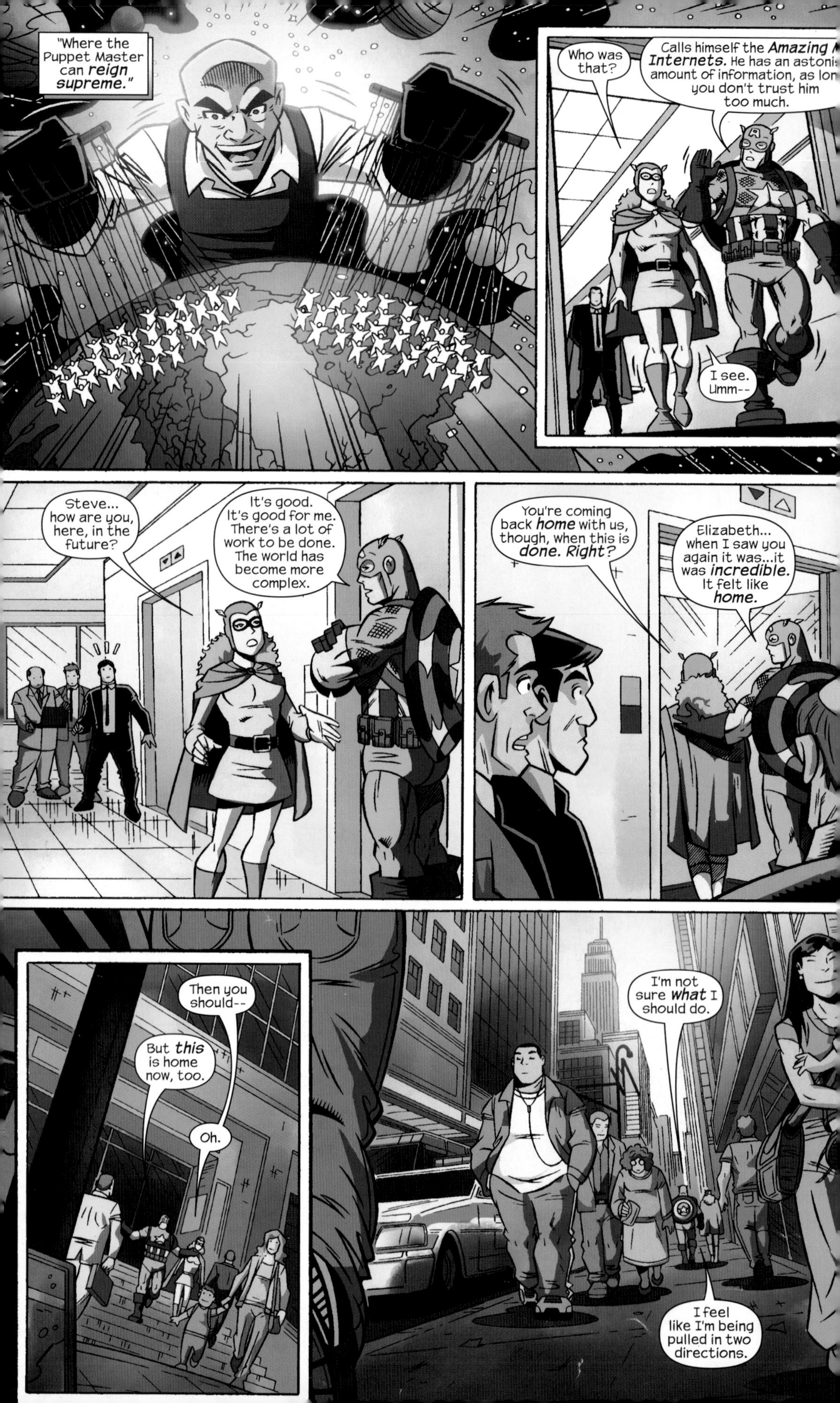

"Where the Puppet Master can *reign supreme.*"
Who was that?
Calls himself the *Amazing* ... *Internets.* He has an astonis... amount of information, as lon... you don't trust him too much.
I see. Umm--
Steve... how are you, here, in the future?
It's good. It's good for me. There's a lot of work to be done. The world has become more complex.
You're coming back *home* with us, though, when this is *done. Right?*
Elizabeth... when I saw you again it was...it was *incredible.* It felt like *home.*
Then you should--
But *this* is home now, too.
Oh.
I'm not sure *what* I should do.
I feel like I'm being pulled in two directions.

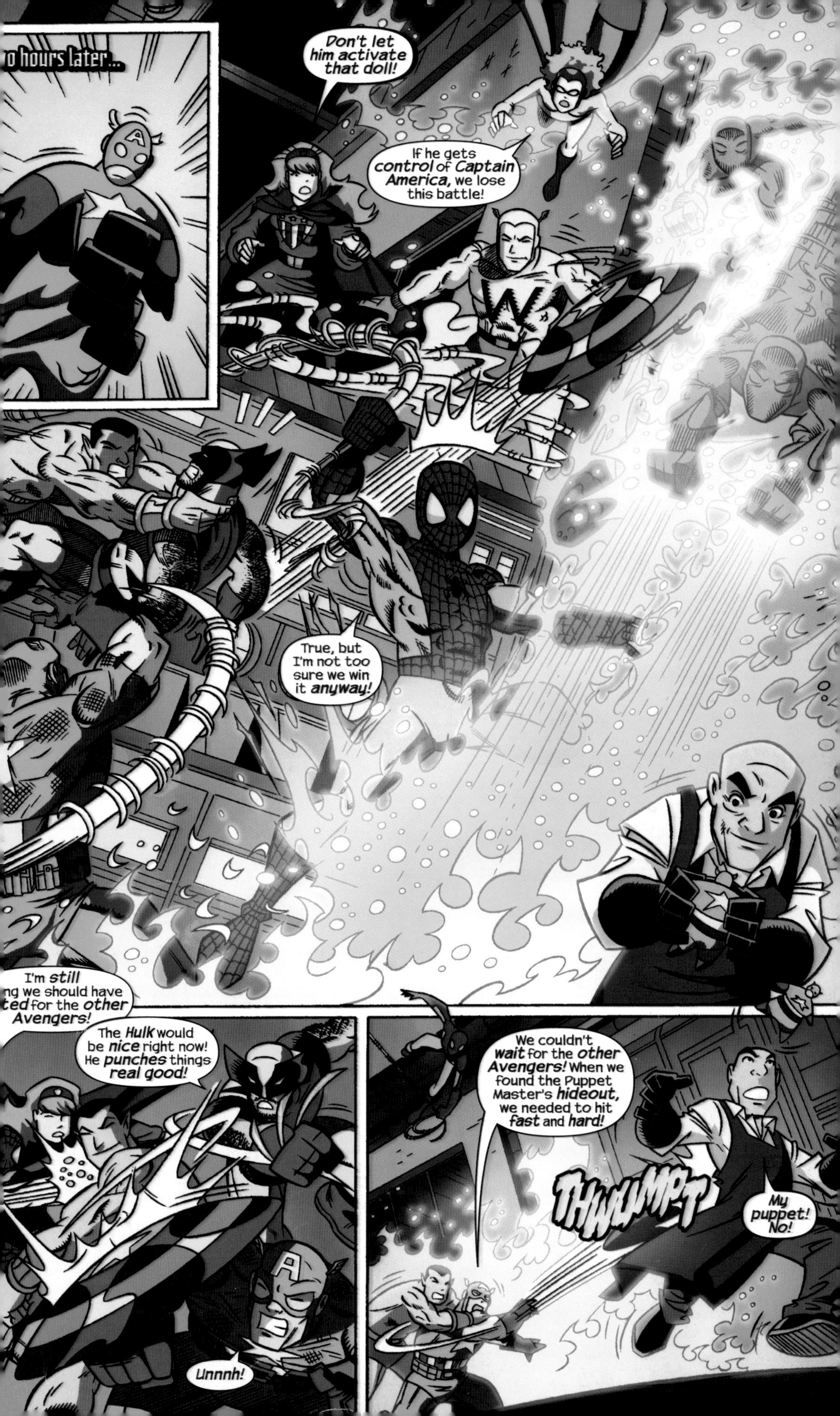
o hours later...
Don't let him activate that doll!
If he gets control of Captain America, we lose this battle!
True, but I'm not too sure we win it anyway!
I'm still ng we should have ted for the other Avengers!
The Hulk would be nice right now! He punches things real good!
Unnnh!
We couldn't wait for the other Avengers! When we found the Puppet Master's hideout, we needed to hit fast and hard!
THWUMPT
My puppet! No!

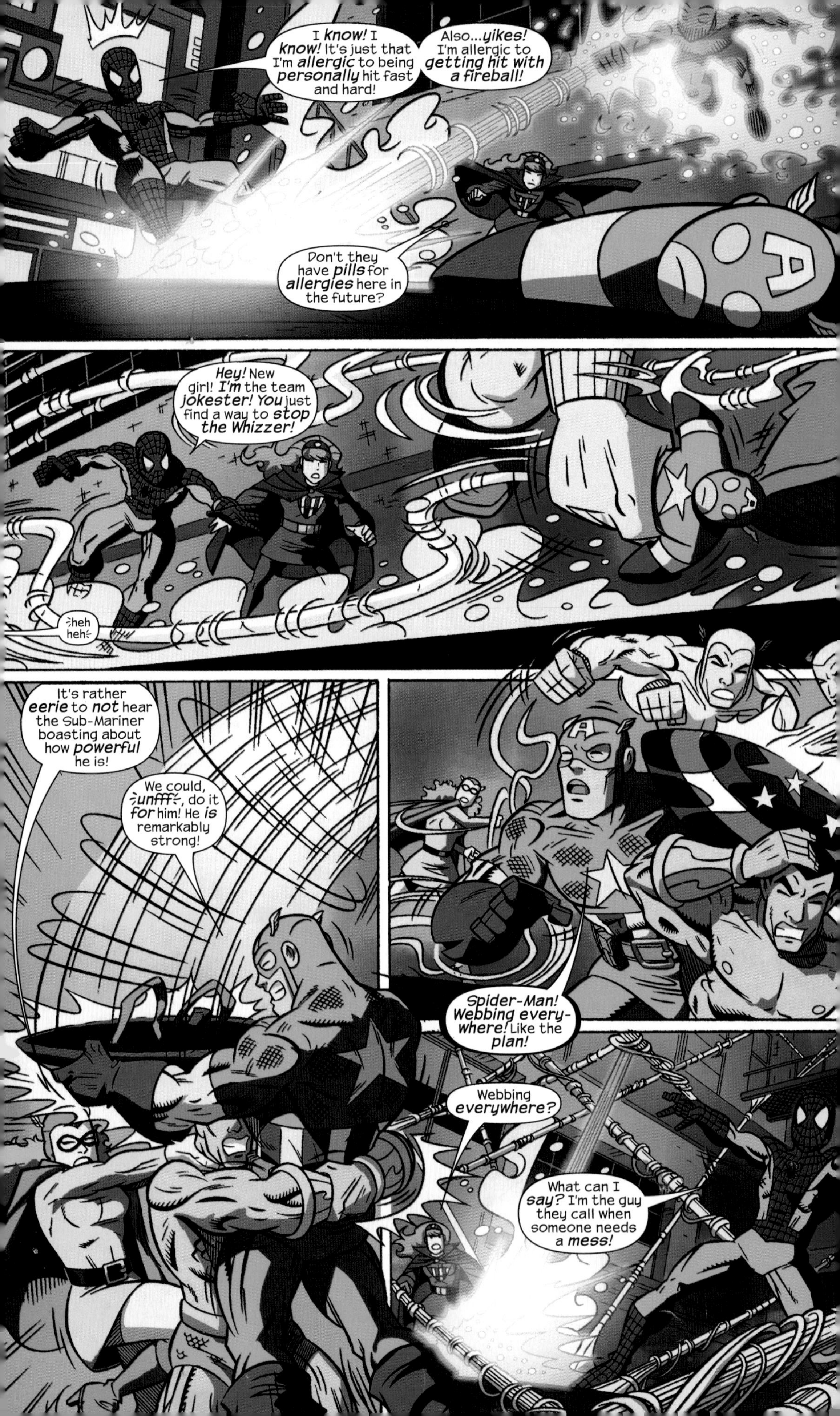

I know! I know! It's just that I'm allergic to being personally hit fast and hard!
Also...yikes! I'm allergic to getting hit with a fireball!
Don't they have pills for allergies here in the future?
Hey! New girl! I'm the team jokester! You just find a way to stop the Whizzer!
heh heh
It's rather eerie to not hear the Sub-Mariner boasting about how powerful he is!
We could, unfff, do it for him! He is remarkably strong!
Spider-Man! Webbing every-where! Like the plan!
Webbing everywhere?
What can I say? I'm the guy they call when someone needs a mess!

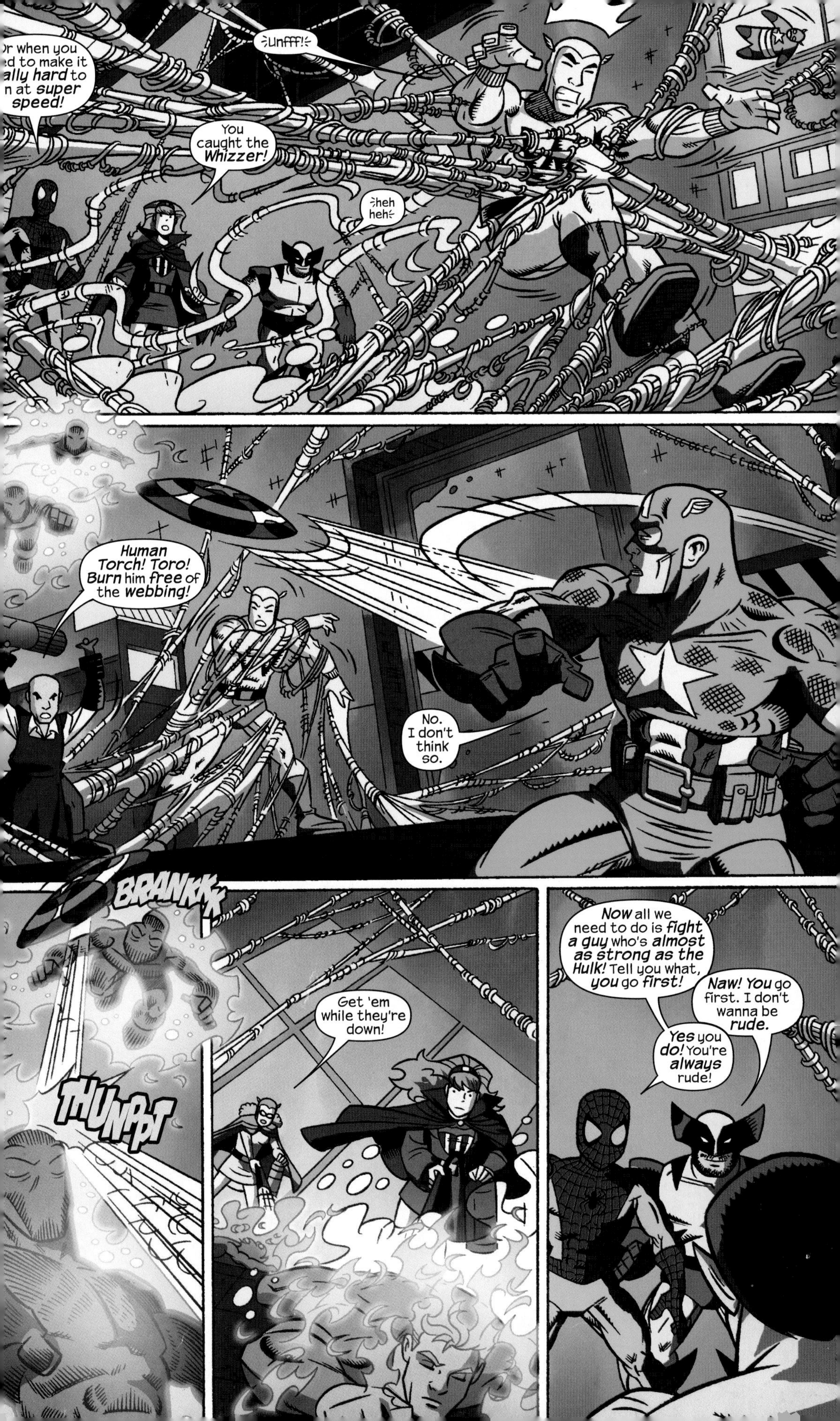

...r when you ...d to make it ...ally hard to ...n at super speed!
Unfff!
You caught the Whizzer!
heh heh
Human Torch! Toro! Burn him free of the webbing!
No. I don't think so.
BRANKKK
THUNPPT
Get 'em while they're down!
Now all we need to do is fight a guy who's almost as strong as the Hulk! Tell you what, you go first!
Naw! You go first. I don't wanna be rude.
Yes you do! You're always rude!

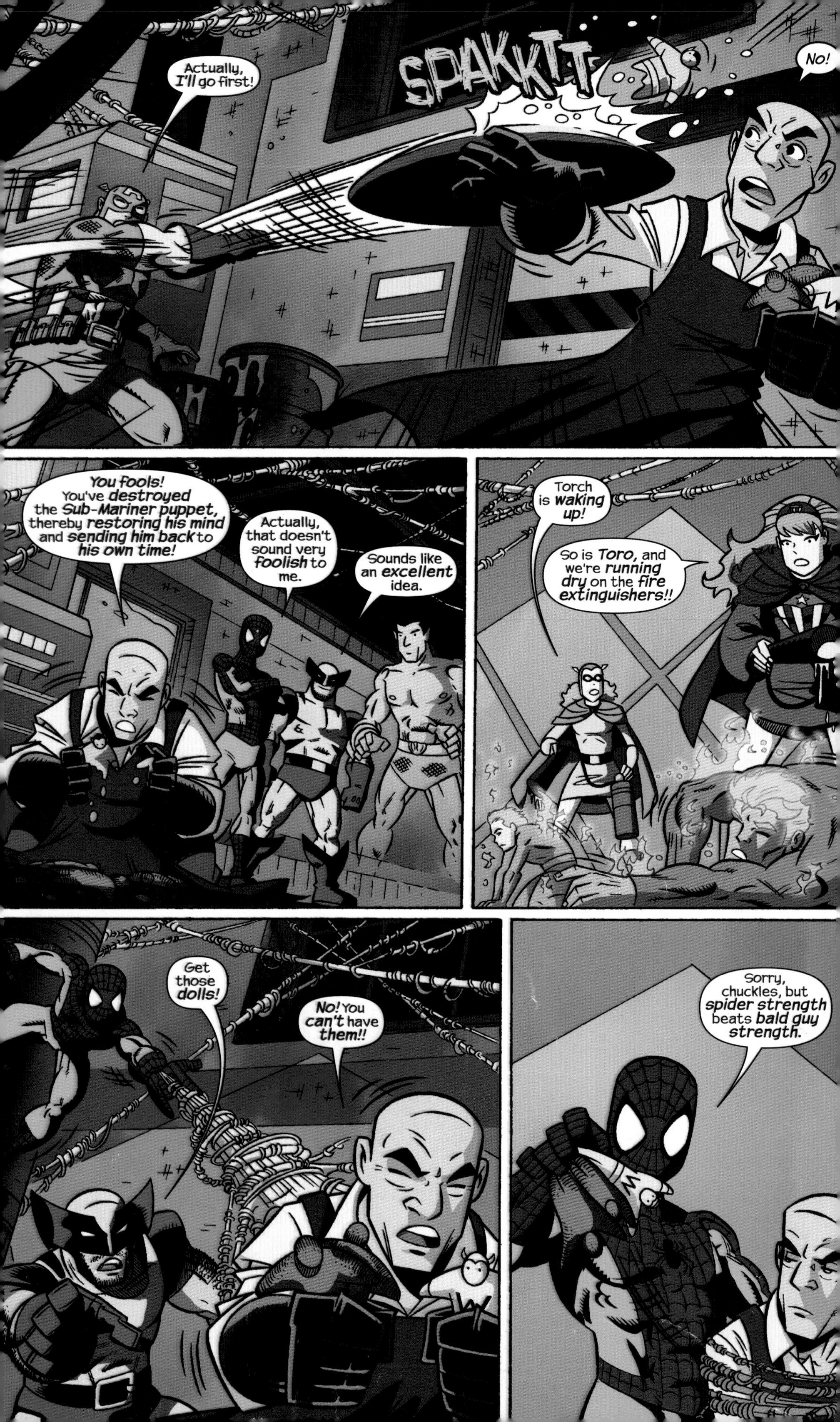

Actually, I'll go first!
SPAKTT
No!
You fools! You've destroyed the Sub-Mariner puppet, thereby restoring his mind and sending him back to his own time!
Actually, that doesn't sound very foolish to me.
Sounds like an excellent idea.
Torch is waking up!
So is Toro, and we're running dry on the fire extinguishers!!
Get those dolls!
No! You can't have them!!
Sorry, chuckles, but spider strength beats bald guy strength.

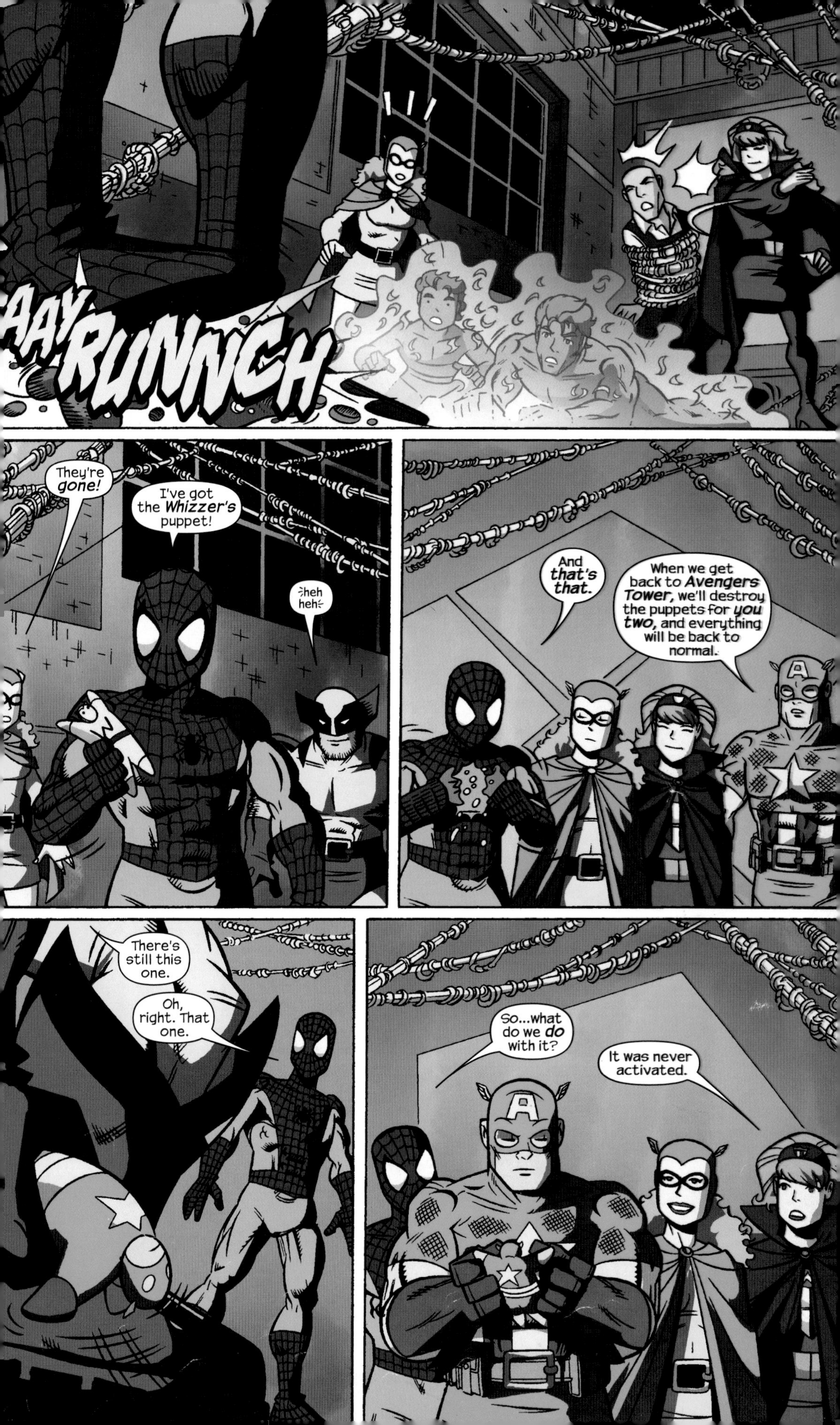
AAAYRUNNCH
They're gone!
I've got the Whizzer's puppet!
heh heh
And that's that.
When we get back to Avengers Tower, we'll destroy the puppets for you two, and everything will be back to normal.
There's still this one.
Oh, right. That one.
So...what do we do with it?
It was never activated.

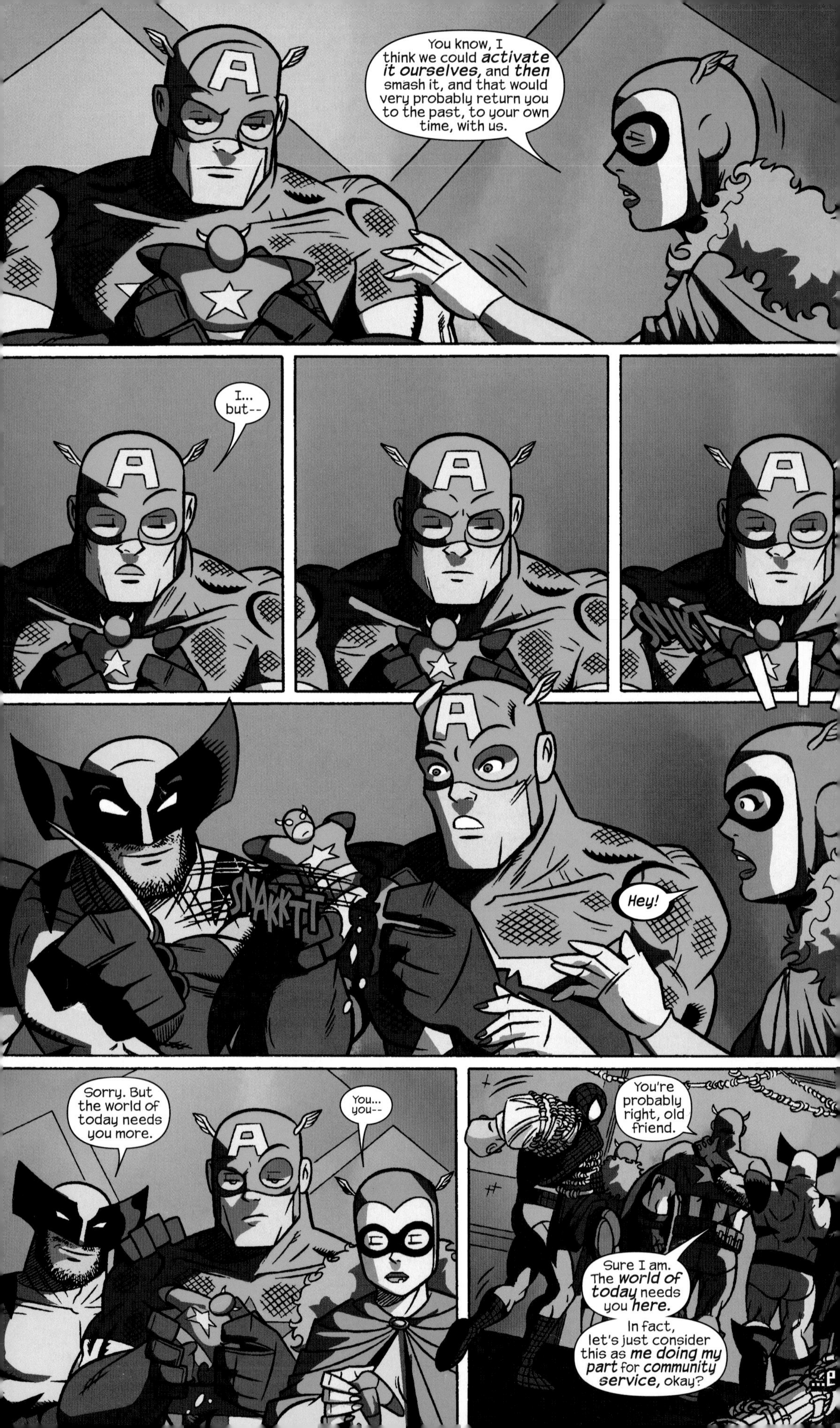

You know, I think we could *activate it ourselves,* and *then* smash it, and that would very probably return you to the past, to your own time, with us.
I... but--
SNIKT
SNAKKTT
Hey!
Sorry. But the world of today needs you more.
You... you--
You're probably right, old friend.
Sure I am. The *world of today* needs you *here.*
In fact, let's just consider this as *me doing my part* for *community service,* okay?